The Mystery of Campion Cave

Contents

Written by Yvonne Cook
Illustrated by Mark Wilson

A Dragon in the Night

"Quick, come here Jordan!" shouted Emily. "There it is again."

Jordan ran outside to join Emily.

"There," Emily shouted again. "Can you see?"

"Over there?" said Jordan, pointing to the sea under the cliffs. "It *does* look like a dragon. But it can't be!"

"Well, if it's not a dragon, what is it?" asked Emily, as they watched the creature glide through the evening mist, heading for the rugged cliffs of Campion Bay.

"I don't know," answered Jordan quietly.

"I told you I wasn't seeing things," said Emily. "Maybe now you'll believe me."

Emily was eight, two years younger than her brother Jordan. Emily often made up stories, but this time she was telling the truth.

"Do you think we should tell Dad?" asked Emily.

"He'd never believe us," replied Jordan. "Anyway, it's gone now."

Emily looked out at the water again. Jordan was right, the dragon had mysteriously vanished.

Before they could talk any more, their big sister, Jana, came through the door.

"Bedtime, you two," she said.

"But tomorrow's Saturday," moaned Emily. Jordan knew there was no point arguing with Jana. Anyway, Jana had already taken Emily by the hand, so Jordan followed the two of them inside.

The Robbery

Jordan was the first to wake up the next day. He got out of bed and went down for breakfast. His mother was reading the newspaper. She looked upset.

"Someone broke into poor Mrs. Lin's house yesterday," she said. "Nothing seems to be missing except her dog, Sparky."

"That's terrible," said Emily, standing in the kitchen doorway. "I bet it was that dragon that did it."

"What dragon?" asked Emily's mother, looking up from her paper.

"The dragon that Jordan and I saw in Campion Bay last night. I bet it eats dogs," replied Emily.

"Oh, really Emily!" sighed her mother. "You read far too many crazy stories."

Then, before Emily could say anything more, Jordan grabbed her by the hand and pulled her out the door.

"We're just going down to the beach," he yelled to his mother. "See you later."

"Don't be long," she called out after them. But they were already running along the path that led down to the beach below.

"Let go of me!" shouted Emily.

"I'm sorry Emily," said Jordan, "but if you really want to solve this mystery, don't go telling everyone about the dragon. They won't let us go out if they really believe there's a dragon at the beach."

"Do you really think the dragon ate Mrs Lin's dog?" asked Emily.

"I don't know," replied Jordan. "But let's try and figure out what it could be."

"I think the dragon would have come up on the beach near Black Rock," said Emily, pointing to a large rock jutting out into the sea.

"If the dragon came up onto the beach last night, there should be some tracks in the sand," said Jordan.

"There're only those tracks over there," said Emily, looking up the beach.

"What tracks?" asked Jordan.

"There, leading up from the water to the cliff," replied Emily excitedly.

"Those tracks look like they were made by the beach patrol," said Jordan.

"But the beach patrol never comes this far down," said Emily. "That's mysterious."

"What's mysterious?" asked a soft voice. They turned around to see a tall, thin man wearing a black wetsuit standing in front of them.

"Nothing," said Jordan, as he grabbed Emily's hand and they ran away.

A Visit to Mrs. Lin's

"Wow, that man was scary," panted Emily, as she and Jordan ran up the rocky path to Mrs. Lin's house.

"Don't tell anyone," said Jordan. "No one! Do you understand, Emily?"

"Yes," said Emily, as they reached Mrs. Lin's.

Mrs. Lin was still very upset when the children arrived at her house.

"Hello, Emily. Hello, Jordan," she said as she opened the door. "Come in."

"We heard about Sparky," said Emily.

"I got such a scare," said Mrs. Lin, "and I'm so worried about Sparky. It doesn't matter about the map."

"What map?" asked Jordan, his ears pricking up. "The newspaper didn't say anything about a map."

"Oh, it was just an old map that used to hang in a frame on the dining-room wall," said Mrs. Lin. "I've only just noticed it's gone."

Jordan remembered the map. They had looked at it many times before. Jordan had even made a tracing of it when they were visiting Mrs. Lin last year.

"Why would a robber want that map?" asked Jordan.

"I don't know," replied Mrs. Lin, fighting back the tears. "I just want my Sparky back."

"Did you see the robber's face?" asked Emily.

"No. I only woke up when I heard the door closing," replied Mrs. Lin. "I looked out the window and saw two people running away. They looked like they were wearing black wetsuits."

Emily and Jordan looked at each other. Black wetsuits! Just like the mysterious man on the beach.

"Will you stay for lunch?" asked Mrs. Lin.

"We'd really like to," replied Jordan, "but we need to get home."

"Thank you, Mrs. Lin," said Emily. "See you later."

Inside Campion Cave

When they got home, Emily made a sandwich and Jordan went to find his tracing of Mrs. Lin's map. He put it under his shirt and ran downstairs. Emily pushed a sandwich into his hand as they headed for the back door.

"Just a minute," called their mother. "Where are you two going now?"

"Oh, nowhere much," said Jordan. "We just want to go exploring down on the beach again."

"Be back by four," said their mother, "and no swimming. You know the rules."

As soon as they were out of sight, Jordan took out the map tracing.

"Look, there's a path marked on the map. It starts near that funny rock by Mrs. Lin's house," he said.

LIN'S

PATH

ROCK

BAY

Emily and Jordan ran as fast as they could up to the rock. It stood in a clearing, jutting up from the ground near the cliffs of Campion Bay.

"Somewhere near this rock is the start of a path," said Jordan, studying the map.

"I don't see anything at all," said Emily. "Maybe the path's overgrown."

Just then they heard a far-off whining noise. It was coming from under the ground.

"Did you hear that?" asked Emily, looking a bit scared. Before Jordan could answer, the sound came again. This time it was louder.

"Follow me," called Jordan, ducking behind the rock. "The path goes down here!"

Jordan pulled a flashlight out of his pocket and flicked it on. Jordan never went out anywhere without his flashlight. In the beam, the children could see narrow steps going down into the rock.

"We're heading into a cave," whispered Jordan, as he led the way. "Stay close to me, Emily." But Emily was already holding on tight to his shirt.

Then they heard the sound again. This time, through the still, cool air, the sound was a long whine, then a faint yelp.

"I know what that is!" said Emily. "It's Sparky!"

Sure enough, a little further on they found Sparky. She had fallen down a hole near the cave entrance. Emily picked her up.

"I wonder what she was doing down here," Emily said.

"I think I know," replied Jordan. "You see, the robbers didn't take Sparky. She chased them as they left the house. She must have followed them down here, then fallen into the hole."

Jordan looked at the map again. "This is the way," he said, pointing to a tunnel leading into a large cave.

"Ouch!" yelled Emily, nearly dropping Sparky. "I just bumped my leg on something sharp."

Jordan shone his flashlight on a stalagmite growing from the cave floor.

"Careful," he said. "Stalagmites take thousands of years to grow. You don't want to damage them."

"I didn't see it," retorted Emily.

Jordan flashed the light around the cave. He flashed on the stalactites hanging from the roof.

"This cave would be cool if it wasn't so cold and scary," said Emily. "Those stalactites look just like giant icicles."

As the children gazed around the cave, a black shape came out of the shadows behind them.

Trapped

"What are you two doing here?" asked a soft voice that they already knew. It was the man they had met on the beach!

"Exploring," said Emily. "Who are you? I think you're the thief who stole Mrs. Lin's map."

Jordan kicked Emily in the darkness. Now they were in deep trouble.

"Oh, do you now?" said the man, moving closer.

"Quick, run!" cried Jordan.

But it was too late. The man reached out and grabbed them. Sparky jumped from Emily's arms and ran off into the dark.

"I'll get your dog later," said the man, as he pushed the children into another rocky tunnel and down a long, narrow path. After what seemed like forever, the man pushed them out into another large cave. In the middle was a dark blue pool of water.

"What are you going to do with us?" asked Jordan.

Before the man could answer, a diver surfaced from the pool. She was busy flipping off her mask and didn't see the children.

"I've got it!" she yelled, holding up a small packet. "I've found the treasure!"

"That's what the map was for!" gasped Emily. "It was a treasure map."

"That's right," said the man. "It led us to a treasure that's been hidden in Campion Cave for 200 years."

"And now it's ours," said the woman, smiling.

"So this is Campion Cave," said Jordan. "I thought Campion Cave and its buried treasure was just an old story."

"Too bad you won't be able to tell anyone about it," said the woman, giving Emily a shove. "You two have a date with a dragon."

"A dragon!" both children said together. Turning round, they saw a huge dragon at the far end of the cave.

"Don't worry," said the woman. "It won't eat you. It's made from plastic and it sits on top of our boat."

"So that's what made the tracks at Black Rock," said Jordan quietly.

"That's right" said the man. "We pull our boat up out of the water onto the land. The dragon's to scare people off. Too bad it didn't work with you two. Now, quickly, get inside."

With that he pushed Emily and Jordan through a narrow door and into the dragon.

He turned a key and the engine inside the dragon roared. Then the woman flicked a switch and the wall of rock in front of them slid open. The dragon moved out of the cave onto the beach.

"We made it," cried the woman loudly. "Tomorrow we'll get rid of these kids and sell the treasure. We'll be rich!"

The Rescue

Just then, a dog barked. "It's that dog again!" hissed the woman angrily. "Someone's out there. Head for the water! Quick!"

"Stop right where you are," said a voice over a megaphone. Jordan saw his chance. Grabbing Emily by the arm, he pushed the door open. The two of them jumped out into the shallow water, then ran for the beach without looking back – straight into their mother's arms.

"We were so worried when you weren't home by four," said their father. "Then Sparky turned up. We knew something was wrong, and then Sparky led us back to the beach."

"We called the Beach Patrol," said their mother. "We'd almost given up hope, and then we saw that dragon thing come out of the cave. When Sparky started barking, we knew you were inside."

The children turned around to see the man and woman being led away by the Beach Patrol.

"Well, I really have a story to tell now!" said Emily. "I'll call it the *Mystery of Campion Cave*!"